Mommy's High Heel Shoes

For Matt,
Tierney, Margaux,
And Philip~

xx

Cupcake
xx Kisses, xx

Kristie Finnan

written by Kristie Finnan

illustrated by Pat Achilles

MOMMY WORKShop BOOKS

MOMMY WORKShop BOOKS · Doylestown, PA · Text copyright © 2008 by Kristie Finnan · Illustrations copyright © by Pat Achilles · All rights reserved · No part of this book may be used or reproduced in any manner whatsoever without written permission except in the case of brief quotations embodied in critical articles and reviews. · For contact information go to www.MOMMYWORKShop.com · Book Design by Heather Weaver · Printed in China · First Edition 10 9 8 7 6 5 4 3 2 1
Publisher's Cataloging-In-Publication Data (Prepared by The Donohue Group, Inc.)
Finnan, Kristie.
Mommy's high heel shoes / written by Kristie Finnan ; illustrated by Pat Achilles. -- 1st ed.
p. : col. ill. ; cm.
Summary: After Mommy leaves for work, her children play with the many shoes in her closet. The story explores the subject of why mothers work and celebrates a working mother's relationship with her children. Hidden pictures are included in each page.
ISBN-13: 978-0-9817565-2-3
ISBN-10: 0-9817565-2-2
1. Working mothers--Juvenile Fiction. 2. Women's shoes--Juvenile Fiction. 3. Working mothers--Fiction. 4. Shoes--Fiction. 5. Picture puzzles. I. Achilles, Pat. II. Title.
PZ7.F566 Mo 2008
[E]   2008905461

I love cupcakes, especially the icing, so my parents call me Cakes.

After breakfast, I ask Mommy, "Can I have a cupcake?" But she says, "No, I have to leave early today. Cupcakes are too messy."

Mommy puts on her high heel shoes
and says, "Cakes, I love you!"

I know it's a work day. Mommy always
wears her high heel shoes to work.

After Mommy kisses me goodbye, I go upstairs and open her closet. I especially love to try on her high heel shoes!

Mommy's high heel shoes are tricky to walk in.

They wobble.

They flip and flop.

Sometimes, they fall off.

Mommy says there are some days she
wishes she didn't have to go to work.
I can see why she says that.
Walking in her shoes is not easy!

So I wonder, why does Mommy wear those high heel shoes?

Maybe her shoes help her climb up huge beanstalks.

Or maybe the giants she works with are famous!

I can't wait to see Mommy after work.
I'm going to ask her about her high heel shoes.

Look at all of these shoes.
I'm going to try on every pair!

Mommy has shoes for...

making waffles in the morning,

watering sunflowers in the garden,

walking the dog in the rain,

shopping for food at the market,

eating cupcakes with friends,

going out to dinner and the movies,

exercising in the living room and playing on the beach.

I even put on the special shoes Mommy wore when we squished through the mud on my school pumpkin patch trip.

Wow! Mommy is so COOL!
She gets to wear all of those shoes.

They must make Mommy's feet feel tired because sometimes I catch her wearing no shoes at all.

Finally, Mommy's home!
She's hiding something behind her back.
I think it's a surprise for me.

She slides a little white box on the table and gives me a GIGANTIC hug and kiss.

Mommy flips her shoes off.
"Do you wear high heel shoes because you work with giants?" I ask.
"No, Silly," Mommy laughs.
"I don't work with giants. I just love wearing fancy shoes."

"But they're hard to walk in," I say.
"Sometimes, but wearing them makes me feel good," Mommy says.
"And when I feel good, I'm a better mommy."

"Why do you wear so many different shoes?" I ask.
"I wear lots of shoes because mommies have lots
of things to do," Mommy says.
"Like taking me to the park?" I ask.

"Yes," Mommy says.
"Like giving me a bath?" I ask.
"Definitely," Mommy says.

"And do you know what my favorite and most important job is?" Mommy asks.
"Buying cupcakes," I say.

"No, Cakes. Being your mommy!"

Mommy hands me the little white box.
Inside are the most beautiful cupcakes!

I give Mommy my biggest, yummiest
and messiest cupcake kiss ever!

On each page you will see a cupcake, ladybug and heart.
Look closely, some are hard to find!